MONTANA RESCUER

HEIRS OF GUARDIAN VALLEY

BOOK FOUR

HALLIE BENNETT

I0619521

Searching for more protective heroes?
Check out the Mountain Men of
Suitor's Crossing series <u>here</u>[1]!

CHAPTER ONE

HOPE GONZALEZ

"I don't get urges to move closer to men—no matter how attractive I find them."

ANOTHER MOAN FILTERS through the wall as I pass Braden's study on my way to the kitchen. Seems like he and my best friend, Carrie, are at it again. Ever since we arrived at his estate a month ago, they've been glued together—love at first sight.

I'm happy for her.

But it doesn't help the stinging envy every time the walls vibrate with the sounds of sex or I witness their playful kisses. Within the past few months, both of my closest friends have found love with men who adore them, though that seems too tame of a word.

Braden and Travis are obsessed with the women in their lives. I read a lot of romance novels—a fair share that includes 'fated mates' or 'instalove'—but I didn't think it could happen in real life until my friends were quickly claimed by their men.

Now, I'm the last single one of the bunch and the only virgin, if the moans and breathy sighs coming from the other room are anything to go by.

Carrie and I used to be two peas in a pod when it came to men. We'd never had boyfriends. Were never-been-kissed virgins.

Until Braden.

Until Brooke suggested we spend time on this massive Montana estate co-owned by Braden and Travis.

With homes for each of them, the ranch provides a quiet retreat from their business travels. Though now that Brooke and Travis are married, they've taken to staying here full-time.

Carrie and I were supposed to stay at Brooke's empty home while she and Travis were away, but the first day we arrived, Braden greeted us at the door and the rest is history. Rather than jetting off to LA for a business deal after welcoming us to the property, he stayed on, taking meetings from home while spending as much time as possible with Carrie.

The two of us ended up at Braden's house instead, since he and Carrie were suddenly joined at the hip, and I didn't want to be alone in Brooke and Travis's huge home.

Bypassing the kitchen, my hunger evaporating with my melancholic thoughts, I grab my coat, tug on my boots, and step outside to get away from the happy couple.

A misty fog hovers over the grounds. The somber gray infuses the October chill with even more bitterness as my breath puffs in clouds of heat before disappearing.

Following the stone path away from the house, I head toward the woods. A few days earlier, Carrie asked Braden if there were horses around here, and he'd mentioned something about them 'being in the back.' It's odd for a stable to be kept so far from the main compound, but what do I know about wealthy men's estates?

Guardian Valley is home to several ranches with plenty of land for horses to roam. Some graze right up to the wooden posts corralling them from the road, like Serenity Ranch a couple of miles down, while others remain hidden behind a forest of trees left as privacy barriers—like this estate and whoever butts up next to it.

Pulling the coat zipper higher over my sweater, I wonder how I'm going to survive the next few months surrounded by lovebirds.

We're spending the last part of the year here since the online magazine Carrie and I run can be managed from anywhere, and we're working on securing a book deal to grow our audience. The picturesque scenery makes for beautiful photos from Carrie and inspiration for my craft projects—which should be my focus instead of lamenting my relationship status.

It would just be nice to be wanted for once.

Hire a matchmaker.

A personal stylist.

Transform yourself into someone new.

The mantra gets shoved aside in favor of reality and the other reason I agreed to live in Guardian Valley for so long—the inheritance bequeathed to me from Mr. Dell Foster, a dead CEO billionaire responsible for the deaths of my parents.

Well, his company plane was responsible.

When the children of those who'd perished in the accident were encouraged to sue Foster after the plane crash, his lawyers found a loophole that saved the man from paying us an exorbitant amount in damages and emotional trauma.

Guess his conscience wouldn't let him die with that black mark in his past, though, so he arranged for those of us he'd cheated to receive an equal split of his entire fortune. As long as we lived in Guardian Valley for a year.

Technically, I could've gone straight to Serenity Ranch—which is part of his holdings—but the coincidence of everything had me searching for solid ground.

Because what were the odds that Brooke, also a co-inheritor, would meet and marry a separate billionaire who happened to own land in the same Montana town as the old man who left behind billions of his own?

Then Carrie met and fell for Braden, another wealthy businessman.

My friends' lives are changing, and our group is growing—first with Travis and Braden, then with the other Foster heirs. It's a lot of new people and circumstances, and I need a quiet place to process it all. A place void of strangers, Braden's presence notwithstanding.

"Twenty-nine years old, and this is what it's come to," I grumble. I feel like I should be handling everything better than I am. Hell, I'm about to be a very rich woman, but piles of money don't ease my anxiety.

An old red barn peeks through the branches ahead, and there's a fence with a gate that I unlatch to pass through. Strange that Braden would mark off the property this way, but maybe it's so the horses can't wander up to the house.

Rain begins to drizzle with increasing frequency, clouding the view through my glasses. Hurrying forward, I struggle with the huge sliding barn door before finally squeezing inside and shutting out the sudden deluge.

The combined smell of hay and animals forms a cozy cocoon.

Growing up in cities, I haven't spent much time in barns, but I like the feeling of nostalgia it gives me. A sense of tradition, old-fashioned values, and hard work. Wooden stalls with black bars across the top form a line down either side of the building. Not every stall is full, but a couple of horses poke their heads over the enclosures.

A black one stamps his hooves as if trying to draw my attention.

"Hey, there," I say quietly, even though we're alone. Speaking above a whisper seems like it would disturb the peacefulness of this place. The horse neighs loudly, causing a laugh to bubble up at my ridiculousness.

"What's your name?" I look around his stall to find a placard or sign but nothing decorates the wood except a thick nail to the side where a bridle hangs. The horse doesn't answer, just stomps his feet again and huffs large gusts of air like one of those angry demon horses in movies. "I suppose it doesn't matter. We can still be friends."

I cross my arms over the edge of the gate. "You're definitely the only friend I can talk to at the moment," I admit before word-vomiting on the poor animal.

Inexplicably, I share my mixed emotions over Carrie and Brooke's relationships and my fears of never having anybody. The sudden inheritance, which isn't much of a consolation prize considering I've been without my parents for two decades.

Hot tears track down my cheeks as everything pours out like a shaken bottle whose cap has finally been released. The weather outside echoes the barrage of words as the rain picks up and pounds across the roof.

The horse must understand my distress because he slowly saunters closer, cautious in his movements, before nudging my head with his own and starting to chew my hair.

A watery laugh escapes as I swipe my hands across my cheeks. "You're a good listener, you know? Sorry, I don't have any treats for you."

"That can be solved easily enough," a male voice rumbles behind me.

I jerk back from the gate and slam a hand to my chest to calm the rapid beating. A man stands inside the stables, his wet slicker dripping water to the dirt floor and forming a muddy puddle. His worn hat lies in one hand as he rakes another through wavy brown hair, and a shiver spreads through my body—from the temperature or his appearance, I'm not sure.

"Didn't mean to startle you, but I wasn't expecting anyone to be out here," he says as he comes further inside until mere feet separate us. Light brown eyes assess me from head to toe, pausing at my face where my ragged emotions are on full display.

"Sorry if it's not allowed. The door wasn't locked, so I thought it'd be okay if I came in." *And I needed to get away from my friends while they had sex.* But that's not something you share with a stranger, especially one who probably works for Braden if he's taking care of his horses.

"Nothing wrong with visiting. You just surprised me. You and Krueger. That horse doesn't calm down for anyone. No one's been able to ride him since he got here, and going near him is asking for a kick. Yet you managed to charm him." A curious note enters his voice before he shifts and motions toward me. "If you want to give him a treat, follow me. We've got the food stored over here."

I consider his offer before following. He doesn't seem dangerous, but being alone with a stranger makes me a little nervous.

Another reason you'll be single forever.

I grimace.

Already an anxious person when it comes to people I don't know, men send my elevated baseline sky high. And it's tough to strike up a friendship, let alone a relationship, when you're too self-conscious to speak.

Swinging open a door, he waves a hand in front of him. "Take your pick."

Sliding past him, I brush against his chest, the smell of male and the outdoors creating an intriguing combination that beckons me closer, but I deny the urge.

My attention flits to the food stores while I shake off the strange notion. This isn't me. I don't get urges to move closer to men—no matter how attractive I find them.

Because they usually don't feel the same way about me.

"Which is his favorite?" I ask.

"Don't know. No one's gotten close enough to risk feeding him a treat from their hand."

"Right... That was a stupid question." I blush and focus on the treat selection. He already said that getting near Krueger would basically land someone on their back.

"Not stupid. You want to know what he likes. Nothing wrong with that."

I glance up to meet his gaze, a warmth tingling down my body as I imagine a double meaning in his words. Like we're talking about *his* likes and me pleasing *him*, which is insanity.

"I'll take a couple of options, so he can choose." Sugar cubes get shoved in my pockets while two apples and carrots fill my hands. "That should be enough, in case he likes one more than the others. You said his name is Krueger?"

Leading me back to the main portion of the stables, the man nods. "Yeah, seemed fitting since he's been a nightmare to handle. His black coat cements the horror theme, though the white socks disrupt the complete image."

"I didn't even notice!" At Krueger's stall, I look down and confirm he has four white socks rising from his dark hooves. He retreats to a corner at our approach, keen eyes darting between me and the man who steps back to give us space.

"Some things haven't changed. He still doesn't like me hanging around."

Setting a carrot, apple, and sugar cube in a line along the lip of the gate, I shrug. "Maybe this will earn you some goodwill. Being around while he gets treats."

"Doubt it, but I appreciate the thought, darlin'."

I duck my head as scarlet heats my skin at the endearment. *It means nothing.* He's a cowboy, rancher, *whatever*, and we're standing in a barn. He probably refers to every woman that way.

"Alright, Krueger, what's your favorite?" The horse stares at me, unmoving. "Come on," I coax, "We brought you treats! Do you like apples? Hmm? Or carrots? They're good for your eyes..." I ramble nonsense until he comes close enough to sniff the line of snacks before snatching up the sugar cube.

"Ah, a sweet tooth. Can't say I blame you." I remove more of the cubes from my pockets, and we spend a few minutes with Krueger's chewing filling the silence. After the sugar cubes, he goes for the apple and carrot, and when everything's gone, I bring a hand to his muzzle, gently rubbing the velvet hair.

I almost forget about the man behind us until he mumbles an awed "I'll be damned."

Shaken from the soothing moment, I step back from the house and face the stranger.

"Thanks for showing me the treats for Krueger. I should probably get going..." I trail off awkwardly, dreading walking home in this downpour. But I can't stay trapped here with him.

"You can't go out in this, especially in those shoes," he gestures to my gray sneakers, "You'll be soaked in a minute."

"I'll be fine. It's just water. I'll dry off when I get to the house."

"And where's that? There's not many people out this way."

"I'm staying at Braden's." It's a weird question since we're on Braden and Travis's estate, but he doesn't know me. I suppose I could be a trespassing drifter.

His jaw clenches at the mention of their names. The lines around his eyes tighten as they narrow, and the immediate air of annoyance is confusing, considering the man's employment under them. I've worked for bosses that I disliked, but Braden and Travis seem nice enough. Though, according to Brooke, before he met Carrie, Braden could be a real jerk.

"I didn't realize Vanderhorn had a woman."

My thighs clench at the growl of his assumption. It sounds so primal being someone's *woman*, though I definitely don't hold that title.

For anyone.

"It's pretty recent... My friend Carrie and I arrived about a month ago, and he's been obsessed with her ever since."

A slight loosening around his shoulders reveals his cooling response, almost like he'd been jealous of Braden, but that doesn't make sense. "Anyway, it's not that far of a walk. Thanks again for your help with Krueger."

I turn to leave before he stops me with a hand on my arm. "Wait, I'll take you."

"Oh, you don't have to do that..."

"I'm taking you," he repeats, "I have a spare rain slicker and hat to protect you. It'll take a minute for me to saddle up Star."

"One horse? I can ride my own."

"Have you ever ridden before?" He removes an oversized black coat and hat from hooks on the wall and hands them to me, their weight surprisingly hefty.

"Once when I was a kid." I shove my arms into the coat. The sleeves go past my fingertips while the hem drags behind me.

Most of the time I don't feel very small despite my 5' 4" stature. I'm curvy, a solid size 20 or 22 depending on the clothing brand, yet this coat manages to make me feel tiny. Buttoning it to my collarbone, I hike up the extra material so I can walk and follow him to where he begins saddling a chestnut horse who neighs in greeting.

"That's not good enough, especially during a storm. The horse could spook, and you'd be thrown off. It's safer to ride with me," he says firmly, hefting a saddle over the horse's back. Doubt creeps over me as I eye it, the man, and me. I'm not sure how the two of us are going to fit on that thing with his burly stature and my curves.

Once all the loops and buckles are checked, he turns to help me up. "Place your foot here, swing over, then scoot closer to the horn. This part." He taps the leather handle sticking up at the front of the saddle.

"I'm riding in front of you?"

"As a precaution. Star's as well-behaved as they come, but in case anything happens, you won't be able to fall off the back."

"You don't have much confidence in my staying on this horse," I joke, though I'm grateful he's thinking of my safety first. Star looks much bigger when I'm standing right next to her, and her intimidating height kindles a nervous ball of energy.

"Better to be safe than sorry. Hold the reins in your left hand and put your right on the pommel here. Your left foot goes in the stirrup." I do as he says as he continues, "You're going to pull yourself up by the pommel and swing your leg over the back. Ready?"

I nod despite my misgivings. If I had to guess, my arm strength is consistent with a spaghetti noodle, but I can't back out now.

He starts counting to three then we're both working to get me up and over, his hands on my waist lifting me with surprising ease. I almost swing over too far, but he catches me, pulling me back to center.

"Perfect," he praises as he removes the stirrup from my foot to replace it with his own. "Hang on."

In a smoother motion compared to mine, he swings up behind me, his hard body pushing me closer to the pommel and horn.

Inappropriate thoughts spring to life as my breathing increases.

Impossible, dirty thoughts.

Leave it to me to skip from virgin to sex on a horse. Maybe I need to take a break from all those books I read. Although to be fair, with all the reading and my vibrator, I don't feel super 'virgin-y'.

"Hold onto this or Star's mane if you feel unsteady, okay?" Warm breath tickles my ear as he leans forward, placing my hands where he wants them.

I can't imagine feeling unsteady with his sturdy presence behind me—not when I'm wedged tight between him and the pommel.

"Okay." The scratchiness in my voice betrays my wayward hormones. Somehow this afternoon turned from me feeling sorry for myself to riding on a horse with a mysterious stranger. A hysterical laugh threatens to erupt at the absurd change, but I rein it in and then chuckle at my pun.

God, I need to get back to my room to escape this dreamscape before I embarrass myself.

With a slight tug on the reins, Star begins walking, and soon we're blasted by watery pellets. The rain shifted to sleet in the past ten minutes, and I'm suddenly very glad to not be walking alone in this.

The borrowed cloak and hat protect most of my skin, but my face still burns with the pinpricks of ice. It almost looks like whiteout conditions with the way my glasses are getting covered.

We meet up with the gate I went through earlier then follow the fence to the right.

"Where are we going?"

"There's not enough room to pass here. We've got to go around to the road." Drops of sleet melt off the brim of his hat and down my collar, before he rocks back again to focus on guiding Star.

The sudden absence of his heat raises the hair on the back of my neck, and instinctively, I push back into his chest, closing the space. His arms tighten their circle around me as my mind wanders into a fantasy of us being stranded in the storm with only our body heat to warm us.

As I near the good part where his mouth starts drifting down my body, we walk up the paved driveway leading to Braden's house. The corners of my mouth lift in a rueful smile at the bad timing, but it's for the best. Back to reality and all that.

We ride up to the wraparound porch where he dismounts behind me. "Here comes the tricky part. You're going to lean forward, swing your right leg back over, and jump to the ground with both feet."

I raise a skeptical brow at the instructions. "You want me to jump from this height?" The ground seems to move further away as I look down, not to mention the slick sheen it has from the sleet.

"Don't worry, I'll catch you. I won't let you fall."

I trust that he'll try, but when I'm barreling towards him, I'm not sure how well he'll be able to stop my momentum. Steeling my nerves, I start to dismount.

"Hope! Where have you been?" Carrie's voice startles me, causing my hand to slip off the horn and send me plummeting toward the ground. My heart jumps to my throat before I slam into a hard chest, which knocks the hat off my head, so I'm immediately soaked in ice water.

"I've got you, darlin'," the man behind me says, and it hits me that I have no idea what else to call him.

"I don't even know your name," I whisper as I try to catch my breath. He steadies me before kneeling to retrieve the fallen hat, shaking it off, and resettling it on my head.

"It's Samuel. Samuel Winters."

I don't have time to respond before Carrie's pulling me away.

"Are you okay? When we couldn't find you in the house, we were worried you were lost in this storm. What were you thinking, and who's that guy?"

I'm bombarded by questions and ushered to the front door. I try to look back to say goodbye to Samuel, but my view's blocked by a jacketless Braden.

He and Carrie must have seen us riding up and ran straight out the door because she isn't wearing a coat either. Maybe that's why there is a harsh look on Braden's face. I caught it before being hurried away, and once again, Braden's and Samuel's relationship confuses me. It seems tense despite working together.

Giving up on speaking to Samuel again, I let Carrie drag me inside and answer her questions. It sucks that we weren't able to have a proper farewell, especially after he rescued me from an icy trek home.

Maybe it's for the best.

Less chance of embarrassing myself by letting my attraction to him accidentally slip.

Sighing in resignation, I remove the borrowed slicker and hat, caress the wet brim with a finger, and then set them aside in the mudroom.

Leaving the evidence of my time with Samuel behind.

CHAPTER TWO

SAMUEL WINTERS

"I'm not about to lose my family's land to another rich man wanting to buy up Montana."

HOPE'S FRIEND DRAGS her away from me, and my muscles twitch from the effort to not tug her back.

Because she's not mine.

And I have to deal with fucking Braden Vanderhorn.

Even his name is pompous, I think, as a grim line of annoyance forms on my mouth.

For the past nine months, he and his business partner, Travis Gibson, have been trying to purchase my property to expand their own. As if fifteen hundred acres isn't enough for them. They don't even keep livestock on the land, preferring to let it sit and showcase their wealth by how much of a getaway from the city they can build.

I've told them time and again that I'm not selling, yet they refuse to take no for an answer.

Harper's Landing has been in my family for over eight decades. Passed down from generation to generation starting with my great-grandpa, Harper, who bought it right after The Great Depression.

I'm not about to break that line.

Though I don't have anyone to leave it to... *yet*.

An image of Hope pops up before I shake it off.

Too much. Too fast.

Those words ring in my head, the death knell from my last relationship.

"How'd you find Hope?" Vanderhorn's question brings me back to the present where the awareness of ice sticking to my exposed face reminds me it's time to get out of this weather.

"She was in the stables, which last I checked is still on my land," I say pointedly, "*She* found *me*."

"And you decided it was wiser to bring her back on horseback instead of driving?" Suspicion coats his words as his eyes narrow.

"I don't answer to you," I grunt, remounting Star. Either way, it would've been tricky getting back here, but I prefer having more control with a horse that's made to withstand the elements than a car that can slide off a slick road.

Besides, I liked having Hope pressed against my front even with the layers of clothing between us.

Too intense.

"When it comes to those under my care, you do," Vanderhorn argues, lowering his crossed arms and clenching his fists. He must be freezing standing out here without a jacket.

It gives me a little satisfaction. Seeing him so uncomfortable.

I don't like the way he claimed Hope, though. Even if it's brotherly concern on his part.

"Best get inside before you lose something important," I warn, tipping my hat mockingly before turning Star back down the drive.

"By the way, my offer still stands. It's more than generous, and you know it," he calls out.

"I told you already Harper's Landing is not for sale." The words are swallowed by the noisy weather, but I couldn't care less if he hears me or not. We've gone over this numerous times, but he refuses to let it go.

He fails to understand the importance of family legacy versus piles of money in my bank account.

My best friend Heath, who co-owns my other neighbor, Serenity Ranch, had his family's legacy sold by his father to a billionaire. Heath lucked out that the new owner turned out to be a pretty woman the wealthy old man had bequeathed it to. Luckier still that Adeline agreed to marry Heath, and they fell in love.

I'm not about to lose my family's land to another rich man wanting to buy up Montana. It's like our beautiful state has become some sort of playground for the ultra-wealthy. A status symbol.

Gibson needs to control his friend.

Travis Gibson seems like an alright guy if I ignore the fact that he's tied to Vanderhorn. We see each other regularly at Serenity Ranch since he's married to one of the heirs, but that doesn't mean I trust him. Not when his business partner keeps hounding me about selling my land.

The sleet picks up its tempo, making conditions even worse on the ride back, but I welcome the cold. Maybe it'll help my simmering temperature. *Annoyance at Vanderhorn. Lust for*

Hope. They combine to create an inferno of heat despite the chilly elements.

The imprint of Hope's body against mine lingers. Earlier, her soft curves made it difficult to remain unaffected, and her absence hasn't done a damn thing to dispel my current case of blue balls.

Fuck, this isn't good.

When I have chemistry with a person, my mind and body give it one hundred percent of their attention. No hesitation. No half-measures.

This rush of heady connection with Hope? I've experienced it before—though not as intensely.

And it's a real bitch to handle because it never ends well for me.

Because if I've learned anything over the past few years, it's that I'm not meant for relationships.

No matter how committed I am.

Besides, running two businesses is enough to keep me busy, and I've finally managed to get our horse training program in the black after some tough financial years. Now's not the time to pull back to make room for a relationship.

Not with Vanderhorn breathing down my neck about selling.

Not over a woman I barely know.

Who'd probably run the moment I showed my true self.

Exhaling a breath of frustration, I try to clear my mind, which means no more thoughts of the curvy woman with a shy smile.

Star slips as we cross back over onto my land, but I easily remain steady atop her.

God, I love this land.

Growing up, my dad preferred our home in the city and let most of the ranch fall into disrepair. He kept the house up-to-date with the bare minimum necessary for the Christmases and summer vacations we spent here, but it never bothered me. I always felt a connection to the shabby farmhouse.

My great-grandfather built it in 1938—a small two-story home created with his own two hands. I smile as I remember the story of how our family came to this land. It was always told by my grandpa with gusto.

His father saw *The Phantom Empire,* a film starring Gene Autry as a cowboy who discovers another civilization under his ranch, and apparently, my great-grandfather became enamored with living out west on his own ranch, despite being born and raised in Detroit.

After saving all he could from his job manufacturing cars, he hopped a train west until he found a spot pretty enough to settle, which happened to be in Guardian Valley, Montana.

The rest is history.

My family's legacy.

Five minutes later, I dismount and finish rubbing down Star before closing up the barn and heading home. The weather has decided to take another wintry turn for October, and this sleet will become snow with the diving temperatures.

Tomorrow is going to be hell getting up to care for the horses, but I wouldn't change my life for anything. Moving here and fixing up the place was just what I needed after Tara.

Damn, I don't want to think about her.

Stomping my boots in the mudroom, I shrug off my slicker, a rain of droplets falling to the hardwood floor. I grab a towel kept by the door for such occasions and mop up the puddle before hanging it up again. Afterward, it doesn't take long to start a fire before struggling to figure out what to do with the rest of my night.

This is always the worst time of day—when I'm done with work and alone with my thoughts. It's too easy to backtrack to the past and lament my current solitude.

Sighing, I preheat the oven for a frozen pizza dinner and sit at the kitchen island waiting for it to beep. Howling winds buffet the windows as the sound of ice pinging against the glass increases. It looks like I got back in time before it picked up.

An image of Hope talking to Krueger creeps into my thoughts. I couldn't hear what she said, but when she turned in surprise, I sure as hell saw the tears streaming down her cheeks. I wanted to sweep her into my arms to offer comfort and protection but didn't want to scare her.

Hell, it scared *me*—the overwhelming urge to go to her when I didn't know her from Eve.

But there it was: an invisible force in my gut tugging me toward her. Thankfully, I'd restrained myself. Redirected the attention to Krueger and his uncharacteristic actions.

He arrived at the ranch after being found on an abandoned property a few towns over. I don't know what happened to him, but he hasn't taken well to me or anyone else, except Hope.

A rueful smile twists my lips as I picture her small stature next to Krueger's height, taming him into a docile companion. I wonder if she'd do the same to me and know instinctively that she could if I let her near enough.

The oven goes off, and I shake that particular yearning off. Like I said, this is why nights suck, too much time to think and dream. Instead, I'm going to eat this pizza and veg out in front of the television while binging *Yellowstone*.

Is it cliché, a rancher watching a fictionalized show about ranchers?

Maybe, but I enjoy the family aspect and admire the determination they have to keep what's theirs. Minus all the corruption, violence, and downright drama.

I definitely don't need that in my life.

CHAPTER THREE

HOPE

"Being buried alive isn't on my bingo card this year..."

I START MY CAR AND wait for it to heat. The windows are foggy, but at least it's no longer icy out, though who knows how long that'll last.

It's been a few days since my little adventure, and honestly, sometimes I question if it was even real considering how fantastical it felt riding through a storm with a hot cowboy intent on keeping me safe.

That night I immediately searched for western romances to add to my Kindle, imagining a chestnut-haired man with brown eyes as the hero in all of them.

Which is ridiculous, I remind myself for the hundredth time. But once my mind latches onto something or someone, it refuses to let go.

Case in point, I harbored a flicker of hope for a crush I had in college—a guy I hadn't seen in years, yet when he responded to something I posted on social media, I imagined a whole story where we met again and fell in love. That is, until he met someone, fell in love, and married *them*.

That shut down those unwarranted fantasies real quick.

Now, my head is happy to insert a new man with fresh possibilities. Like I'm playing freaking Whack-a-Mole with any random guy who shows me attention.

Not entirely true.

I don't cling to every guy who has ever been nice to me, just the ones I find immensely attractive. Intriguing.

And Samuel is definitely those things.

Shoving an image of the gruff rancher out of mind, I turn my wipers on to clear the windshield of melted frost and decide it's good enough for the drive into town.

I don't have a lot of time to finish my shopping today, since the forecast is calling for snow, but those things are never exact, right?

Should've bought everything online.

Carrie's birthday is this weekend, and I want to go all out for her thirtieth. I don't have a family to celebrate, so showering friends with love and gifts is the next best thing.

However, maybe this time, I should've opted for the easy shipping option versus supporting local businesses as the car cruises down the drive to the main road, which is really an old two-lane highway that hardly anyone uses, instead choosing to take the major interstate that cuts through Guardian Valley.

A sign for Harper's Landing crops up to my right, and I'm reminded again of Samuel and the embarrassing realization that he does not, in fact, work for Braden.

After explaining to Carrie what had happened while Braden listened in, he'd corrected my assumption that Samuel was some kind of ranch hand or stables manager. Which meant I'd trespassed on the man's land and forced him to go out of his way to return me to where I belonged.

I wince again at my mistake and direct my attention back to the road. Nothing I can do to change what happened now.

Samuel has probably forgotten all about me anyway...

Guardian Valley is a cute small town that I'm sure Hallmark would try to emulate if they knew it existed. As it stands, it barely warrants a mention on the map, despite I-90 running through it.

It's unfortunate because once you drive the five minutes to reach its downtown area, Guardian Valley sucks you in, especially during the holiday season.

Which may be year-round judging by the current decor on Main Street.

The shops are lined with lit garlands, the real kind that saturates the air with the fresh scent of pine. Every square inch of space houses pumpkins, twinkling lights, and the friendliest witches and ghosts I've ever seen in honor of Halloween.

After crossing the last item off my list two hours later, I load the wrapped presents and decorations into my trunk and prepare to head home. Thick snowflakes melt on my skin and dot my glasses, and as I look around, I realize I must have been in the antique store longer than I thought because a layer of white covers the street and my car.

Apprehension settles in my stomach, but I remind myself that it's just a little snow, not a blizzard. As I get further away from town, though, conditions worsen, and I regret even thinking about a blizzard.

Shouldn't red and orange leaves be floating on a gentle breeze? Why is it freaking snowing this hard in October? This is not the autumn I signed up for.

Visibility drops to nearly zero as I turn off the radio like that will help me concentrate better. Hunching over the steering wheel, I push the wipers to go as fast as possible, but they struggle to keep up with the snowflakes that seem to have doubled in size in the last ten minutes.

Stay calm, you're okay. Drive slow, and you'll be fine.

My heart is beating out of my chest. My anxiety rising in exact correlation with the falling temperatures outside. Thoughts of colliding with an oncoming vehicle or hitting a deer crossing the road whisk through my brain.

Would a deer be out in the open during a snowstorm?

Oh my god.

I'm dumber than a deer who is smart enough to know to stay sheltered when snow is predicted.

Calm down, you're spiraling.

A random coping method pops into my head, but it's hard to remember all the steps when I'm literally driving in a snow globe. I shift my foot across the pedal, letting up on the gas to slow down more, but the wet rubber sole slips and hits the brake, causing the car to jerk and then swerve.

I lift my foot completely off the pedal, hoping the car will correct itself, but we keep sliding until there's a dip, and the car slams into a ditch. My body lurches forward before it's yanked back by my seatbelt, the edges cutting into my skin. The airbag deploys, bursting in my face like a freaking punch from a professional boxer, sending my glasses askew.

"Ow..." I groan.

I'm leaning towards the right at this angle, and my purse and phone lay on the floor of the passenger side.

Adrenaline courses through my veins and overloads my system, so all I can do is sit here even as I'm being buried by the storm outside.

Time passes slowly, and I think of the times I fell off my bike as a kid. Laying flat on the blacktop. Fighting to catch my breath and feeling like I was dying instead.

Eventually, my fight or flight kicks in, and I manage to turn the keys so the car turns off. Wouldn't do to die of carbon monoxide poisoning, right?

Much better to succumb to freezing temps, I laugh to myself, a sense of panic settling in.

I give myself another minute to feel scared then gather my courage and make a plan. What do those survival skills shows say to do in a situation like this? Stay in the car and wait to be found? Or venture into the unknown and increase your chances of running into someone?

A huff of frustration fills the car. How am I supposed to remember important life-saving tips in the middle of needing my life saved? My brain has gone to mush with all the firing synapses!

Snow completely covers the windows as I twist to look in the back. *That's it, decision made.* Being buried alive isn't on my bingo card this year, so I unbuckle my seatbelt, stretch to get my things, and attempt to open the door.

The heavy weight hardly budges, especially at this angle with gravity keeping it shut. I maneuver around until I can push out with my feet, which brings down an avalanche of freezing snow.

A short scream escapes before I spit out snow and wipe off my glasses. *Stupid, terrible vision!* It's bad enough I can't see in regular conditions, now it's near impossible with blurred lenses that I can't clean properly in the middle of a blizzard.

Get it together, Hope.

My legs bend again to shove at the door until it swings wide enough to balance straight up without tumbling back into my face. Maneuvering around the deflated airbag and steering wheel, I crawl out.

My unprotected hands sink into a mountain of snow. Glancing around, the dark blur of the road stands out but not much else. I slip and fall a few times before my feet feel steady beneath me, and I begin walking in the direction of Braden's home.

It can't be too far. As long as I stay straight, I'll see his driveway and be safe in no time. Piece of cake.

So, I trudge forward singing that old song from *Santa Claus is Comin' to Town.*

"Put one foot in front of the other," I sing, "And soon you'll be walking out the door!"

If anyone saw me at this point, I'm sure they'd have me committed, but you do what you have to to survive. The weatherman called for snow. Pretty, white, not-dangerous *snow.* Not a sudden killer blizzard!

Soon enough, a mailbox covered in snow appears in my hazy vision—a man-made contraption instead of a spindly tree! A shout of glee erupts as I raise my fists in victory.

"Yes!"

I made it.

I actually made it.

Racing ahead, I'm immediately brought back to Earth as my feet slide out from under me, and I slam onto my back.

"Right. Can't run. Slick ground," I mutter.

Rolling to my knees, I carefully stand and follow the slightly raised drive until a small white-washed home comes into view—one that doesn't belong to Braden.

It'll have to do.

Because, at this point, I need heat before losing a finger or toe, so I pray a serial killer doesn't live here and raise a fist to knock on the door.

CHAPTER FOUR

SAMUEL

"...she needs heat, not my roving hands."

THE WHISTLING WIND outside is magnified in my suddenly quiet house. The power went out a few seconds ago, leaving me in dwindling light and quickly fading heat. Thankfully, this isn't my first rodeo, so a stack of chopped wood stays on the porch for such occasions.

Grabbing my coat, I zip it closed before opening the door and finding Hope prepared to knock.

"What the hell are you doing out in this?" I ask while pulling her inside. She's covered in white flakes that swiftly disintegrate into a wet puddle at her feet.

"M... my car... I s... slid off the r... road," she explains through chattering teeth.

I need to warm her up. Fast.

"Are you hurt?" I run my hands down her arms, reassuring myself that she's alright, when I notice red marks creeping below her neckline.

Lifting a hand, I lightly trace the track of bruises as Hope shivers, and I'm reminded that she needs heat, not my roving hands.

"I'm fine. The seat belt and airbag probably left a mark, but otherwise, I'm good." She gently palpates her cheeks as I guide her to the master suite. What I assumed was redness from the wintry air is also, apparently, the residual effects of being blasted by an airbag.

"You can change into these." I drop a pair of sweatpants and a sweatshirt on the bathroom counter after snagging the warm fleece from my dresser. "Unfortunately, the power went out right before you arrived, so we'll have to make do with the dark. I'm going to start a fire for heat. If you need anything, just holler."

Hope nods, and I retreat to the living room. It's the afternoon, but with the heavy snowfall and zero lights, darkness has descended on the room, blanketing it in cool shadows. The short trek between the front door and the pile of firewood on the porch leaves me covered in white.

When the ranch profits increase more, there is going to be a new addition to the house—specifically, expanding the mudroom to house firewood rather than the narrow space it currently is.

The fire crackles merrily in the fireplace by the time Hope eases to the blanketed floor next to me. Holding her hands out to the warmth, she murmurs, "This is nice."

"It should do the trick. If not, I'll start the generator." I probably should've thought to get it running earlier once Hope appeared. She deserves more than a measly fire after surviving a car accident and journeying through a blizzard.

"Actually, I'll go start it—"

"No, it's okay. I'm happy with the fire." Her hand lands on my forearm and squeezes, stopping me from getting up. Sweat breaks out on my forehead, and it has nothing to do with the blaze next to us.

It's an innocent touch.

Nothing innately sexual about it.

Yet the feel of her soft palm wrapped around my arm has my cock rising to attention as I imagine Hope circling another part of my anatomy.

I haven't been able to stop thinking about her from the moment I left her with Vanderhorn, so now my treacherous body aches for my dreams to become reality.

"Are you sure? It's no trouble." And maybe dealing with the generator will give me enough time to get my body under control.

"Positive. The fire is cozy." She smiles, drawing her knees to her chest. My Montana University sweatshirt looks good on her—the maroon coloring practically makes her skin glow.

Searching for anything to get my mind off the escalating need to touch her, I latch onto the first topic that comes to mind. "So, why are you in Guardian Valley?"

She glances out the window before peering back at me, her glasses reflecting the dancing flames of the fire.

"For work. My friend and I run an online magazine for crafters. Carrie handles photography and marketing. I write the articles and instructions along with creating the crafts."

"We came here to work on a special coffee table book because it's on our bucket list to be traditionally published." Excitement emanates from Hope's voice as she animatedly waves her hands around as she speaks.

"People think crafting means kindergarten activities or tacky projects made in five minutes, but our goal for the book is to showcase the nostalgic elegance of homemade crafts. Reminiscent of antique brooches or historical quilts. All of those things we keep protected in museums were crafted, but no one thinks of them that way."

"Sounds like an impressive undertaking," I say, enamored with her passion. *So different from Tara.* My ex's emotions usually hovered between moderate annoyance and moderate pleasure.

Everything in moderation.

At first, I appreciated her ability to coolly navigate life and business—she was an exceptional attorney—but it quickly became obvious how mismatched we were.

Because I expected us to spend more than two nights a week together.

Because I wanted her to let me know when she got home safely after a late night at work.

And it was *too much. Too intense.*

You're too clingy, she said when we broke up. *You're suffocating me.*

So, I shut down. Focused on building the horse training business rather than my shortcomings. Horses don't mind when you check on them; they welcome attention.

"Are you okay?"

The gentle question jerks me out of the past, and I curse my wayward thoughts. I'm over Tara—realized I never loved her as I thought a long time ago—but the wounds she inflicted still like to rear their ugly heads every once in a while.

Especially around Hope.

Because of the obsessive desire I feel for her. The intense need to protect and care for her is a thousand times worse than it ever was with my ex.

And that doesn't bode well for my peace of mind.

CHAPTER FIVE

HOPE

"I'm not cut out for Montana weather."

"SORRY FOR THE BORING explanation. Sometimes I get so caught up in talking about the magazine and book that I forget other people don't care nearly as much as me."

Samuel had zoned out somewhere in my rambling, his glazed eyes not really seeing me anymore.

Of course, the moment I have a man alone, I bore him to death rather than impressing him with sparkling wit. My body isn't enough to capture his attention either, since it's hidden beneath his baggy clothes.

Okay, baggy might not be the right term because they're not exactly hanging off me, but they're definitely turning my roundness into a boxy blob. And no man ever got turned on by those two descriptors.

Boxy blob.

It is kind of fun to say, though.

"Don't apologize for being passionate. I think what you're doing sounds amazing." Samuel smiles, revealing deep dimples that soften his gruff exterior.

"Thanks... But enough about me. What about you? I'm embarrassed to admit that I thought you worked for Braden. I figured I was still on his land when I wandered into the stables."

He clenches his jaw and a rumble of annoyance comes from his chest. "If he had his way, it would be. He's been hounding me about selling the property ever since he moved in next door."

I knew Braden could be persistent when it came to business, and according to Brooke, he could be a real asshole to people. Except Carrie. And me, by extension.

"My family has owned Harper's Landing for generations, and I don't plan on selling it. Ever. Especially not to a bored businessman looking to expand his portfolio," Samuel says, grimacing at the possibility. No wonder I sensed animosity between the two that first day.

"Have you explained that to Braden? He doesn't seem like an unreasonable man."

"I've told him multiple times. He's aware of how precarious the ranch's finances are. We're on better ground now that the horse training business is profitable, but we're a long way off from having a safety net beneath us if anything disastrous hits. Braden is like a shark sniffing out blood in the water."

"I'm sorry." I don't know what else to say. It's not my place to interfere with Braden's business, even if I do feel defensive on Samuel's behalf.

Maybe I can ask Carrie to mention something...

Samuel snags another blanket off the recliner he's leaning against and unfurls it to drape it over my bent knees. "It's not your fault that your friend's boyfriend is a thorn in my side." He changes the subject. "Are you warm enough? Do you want hot cocoa or anything?"

"No, I'm good. I'm just glad I found your place. It was getting dicey out there." I laugh, but it sounds as hollow as it feels.

I'm not cut out for Montana weather.

Freak blizzards are not something I'm equipped to survive. *Except you* did *survive.* How am I supposed to live on Serenity Ranch for a year like I'm Annie Oakley rather than orphan Annie before she meets Daddy Warbucks?

"What do you know about Serenity Ranch? They're your other neighbor, right?" Might as well suss out more information about the place I'll be calling home as soon as I work up the courage to drive over there and announce myself.

I don't know why I'm so hesitant. Maybe because it'll be the first time I've seen the other kids affected by the plane crash since the accident? Maybe I'm subconsciously afraid of digging up that part of my childhood.

"Yeah, I've known the Mannings for years. Heath is a good friend, and his sister is cool, too. Their family owned the land for decades, like mine, until their dad sold it to another billionaire CEO."

"The hills seem to be crawling with them around here," I remark. Isn't there a study about where wealthy people congregate or something? Because Guardian Valley would be on the map.

Samuel chuckles. It's a deep thundering sound that sends a pleasurable shiver down my spine. Forget about blankets and blazing fireplaces, all I need is this man's growly voice to warm me up.

"No kidding. That's another reason I'm opposed to selling to Braden. Even if we were suffering financially like the Mannings were, I'd rather sell at a loss to someone who wants to work the land. Build a home, not an expensive playground for their time off from jet-setting around the world."

"That makes sense." The peaceful surroundings and small-town charm are suited for raising a family. It's a community where a person can put down roots and become connected.

I hadn't considered that aspect of Guardian Valley before, but it's something I yearn for. A sense of belonging.

I thought I might find that in a person—preferably a husband—but with zero relationship experience, perhaps I should consider Guardian Valley a permanent home and start planting the seeds for a thriving future.

A place I can create the supportive, loving life I crave.

It doesn't hurt that I could also keep seeing Samuel, too.

"It's only you out here?" I ask, curious about his personal life. He doesn't wear a ring, so I doubt he's married, but he could have a girlfriend stashed somewhere.

"Yep. My parents retired to Florida three years ago, though they never loved spending much time here. Too rustic."

"The no power thing does kind of suck," I tease. We've inched closer to each other, and I'm chalking it up to sharing body heat.

Yeah, right. You just want to feel the strength of his arms wrapped around you again.

But I'm not exactly a seductress.

"Makes for a cozy time by the fire, though." The back of Samuel's hand grazes my cheek.

That's an opening, right? He broke the ice by touching me, now I need to reciprocate by being brave.

Oh my god, what am I doing?

CHAPTER SIX

HOPE

"Cue my inner seductress."

MY EMOTIONS ARE GOING haywire as I fight nerves—the excited and terrified kind. This is when the heroine in the books I read would scoot closer and take charge of her destiny.

She'd courageously lean forward and—

Oh, thank goodness! The decision is taken out of my hands by Samuel pressing his lips to mine.

It's chaste. A testing of the waters.

"I haven't been able to stop thinking about you," he rasps.

"Really?"

"You're a beautiful woman with a kind heart. I didn't stand a chance."

"What about you? Handsome cowboy to the rescue? Not once but twice!" I hold up two fingers to punctuate the point, though I'm not sure how well he can see them considering how close we are. "A woman can't resist that combination. I even downloaded a bunch of cowboy romances to compensate."

"You did." It's a statement rather than a question as Samuel's chin dips, his lips skimming along my jawline. "Tell me about them."

Inhaling a whiff of his spicy scent, I wrack my brain for story details, but it's completely blank, so I improvise and start narrating what I'd like to happen between us.

Now.

Cue my inner seductress.

Channel all of my favorite heroines.

"Well, they all have gruff cowboys, obviously, and the heroines are on the curvier side."

"Naturally." Samuel's mouth grazes my neck after whispering in my ear. His beard scrapes across the delicate skin to elicit an immediate reaction below as I press my thighs together.

"They're pretty steamy, too." Slowly, my hand settles on his thigh and squeezes the hard muscle, drawing a hum of approval from him.

"Like this?" His hand drags through my hair before landing on the back of my neck, capturing it in a loose hold.

"A little steamier."

A grin toys around his lips, and his rough palm slides lower to cup my breast. "How about now?"

"That's good," I whimper, enjoying this sexy turn of events. "But they're usually hotter. Hot enough to melt my reading device."

Unerringly, Samuel continues his teasing journey until it stops where I've been craving his touch all along—my aching pussy. He presses the seam of my sweatpants into the cleft before clicking his tongue.

"I doubt those books left our girl clothed, hmm? If I were the cowboy in question, I'd need my girl's sweet cunt free from restraints."

His eyes meet mine in a silent question of permission, and I nod. No way am I chickening out. This is the most amazing thing that's ever happened to me, and we've barely started.

Samuel tugs on the elastic waistband, and I awkwardly wiggle out of the warm fleece, pulling my sweatshirt overhead, too. Left in my bra and panties, I don't feel as nervous as I'd expect as a virgin about to have sex with a practical stranger.

Instead, a wave of sensual confidence rises to the forefront, especially when Samuel groans after eating me up with his heated gaze. His clothes quickly disappear and leave a bulk of exposed muscle behind, a sight that has me salivating.

He's not gym-rat fit.

He doesn't have a six-pack, but it's clear his body has been honed by years of doing manual labor.

"You are so gorgeous, baby." Samuel softly kisses the center of my chest and nuzzles the valley between my breasts.

"You're not so bad yourself." I quickly toss my glasses on the couch behind me then dig my fingers into his biceps.

Being in Samuel's arms again is like coming home. We may not know each other well, but he gives off an aura of safety, and I feel protected in a way I never have before.

Maybe it's because he's literally rescued me twice, but there's also something about him that says 'natural born protector,' and it turns my insides to mush.

As one, we lay down on the blanket in front of the blazing fire. The logs spark and crack with each flame while the weather outside batters the farmhouse siding. A storm of elements surrounds us, but the bubble we're in? It's a cozy buffer against everything outside.

"You set the pace, Hope," Samuel says, sincerity shining in his eyes. "You went through a traumatic experience earlier, so we don't have to rush anything. I'm content with holding you like this if that's all you're up for."

Grabbing his hand, I return it to my pussy and prompt him to push harder. "I promise this is what I want. If you knew the dreams I've had—" My sentence remains unfinished as his palm rocks against my fabric-covered clit.

Damn, these panties have got to go.

"I'd like to hear about those dreams, sweetheart, but first, my tongue's dying for a taste of your sweet little pussy. Can I lick you, baby? Please?" The desperate words vibrate along my round belly as he scoots lower until his face hovers over my core.

"Yes..." My hips lift in encouragement, and that's all Samuel needs. With a growl, he dives in to suck my clit through the wet cotton, and I gasp at the electric contact.

Burying my hands in his hair, I moan and pull on the strands, eager for more, which he gladly gives me, plunging two fingers into my clenching channel.

A rip rings through the air as the tatters of my panties leave me completely bare for the onslaught of Samuel's mouth and fingers.

"Fuck, baby. You remind me of strawberries in the summer, warm and sweet, juice dripping down my chin with each bite. I can't get enough."

Neither can I.

It's like I've become a wild woman bucking beneath Samuel's expert tongue. My orgasm is barreling forward in record time, and its intensity scares me. Sure, I've had orgasms in the past, thanks to my trusty vibrator, but this feels different.

What Samuel is building within me feels earth-shattering.

And it is.

With another flick of his tongue, and a twist of his fingers, I come for him, arching into a ray of light and pleasure. He continues devouring me with hungry little growls, easing me from one climax to another, until I whimper and push him away.

A nap is calling my name as contented warmth seeps into my bones, but I fight off the temptation to sleep.

We're not done yet.

CHAPTER SEVEN

SAMUEL

"Hope could be my future."

A PART OF ME WONDERS if I'm dreaming.

If the lost power and raging storm have catapulted me into some sort of dreamland where a girl like Hope wants a man like me—a hardworking rancher who can be overprotective and downright ornery at times.

But this feels real.

Hope's hands combing through my hair. The taste of her sweet arousal on my lips and tongue. How her hips rise to meet my hard cock as I kiss my way back to her mouth, making sure to stop at her breasts to lick and suck the swollen nipples.

"Samuel..." she groans, and my name has never sounded so good.

"Say it again."

She does, and a shudder rolls down my spine to settle in my cock. Nudging between her splayed thighs, our gazes connect as I slowly push forward until I'm buried to the hilt in Hope's tight cunt.

My heart pounds in my chest. Blood whooshes in my ears. This past week has been filled with thoughts of Hope no matter how hard I tried shoving them away. The ghost of Tara's words replayed through my mind, mocking each obsessed daydream.

"Hey, where'd you go?" Hope's hands hold my face still as she searches my expression.

Fuck. Here I am buried inside her warmth, yet I'm frozen in the past.

"Nowhere that matters." My hips retreat then thrust forward, steadily increasing my pace. "I'm here, baby. I'm with you."

Her look of doubt guts me. Reaching down, my fingers find her clit as I capture her mouth in a hard kiss. I want Hope's full attention on pleasure, not worry.

I swallow her gasp of surprise then growl in satisfaction as her pussy clenches around my cock with her orgasm, drawing my own to the forefront.

Collapsing to the side, I fight to catch my breath as Hope curls into me, her head resting on my chest.

"Ready to share what happened?" she asks.

"I'm not sure it's a good post-coital conversation," I joke, ashamed by my brief loss of focus.

Tara is my past.

Hope could be my future.

She deserves one hundred percent of me one hundred percent of the time.

"Let me be the judge of that." Hope pats my chest. "How about we make a trade? A secret for a secret."

"Hmm... I'm intrigued. What sort of secrets are you keeping?"

"Only one way to find out, so spill."

It's obvious she's not going to let this go, and if I have any chance at a future with her, I'll have to share my past eventually. Might as well be now while we're snowed in.

"Relationships aren't my strong suit," I admit. "I know this is new, and maybe you're not interested in more than a—"

A finger lands on my lips. "I'm interested. Don't let this stop you from sharing, but I was a virgin until a few minutes ago."

"What?" Shock reverberates through my body. Hope was a virgin? "Did I hurt you? Why didn't you tell me?" She didn't act like I figured a virgin would. Didn't look like she was in pain when I first entered her. She pulled me closer with each deep plunge of my dick rather than tensing up and asking me to slow down.

"No, you didn't hurt me. Everything was perfect. I didn't mention it because it didn't matter. Which is why I didn't bring up birth control either. I'm on it for my period, by the way." Hope peppers kisses over my pecs before rising to meet my eyes. "I wanted you to be my first, and nothing was going to deter that."

An unexpected chuckle bursts free at the fierceness in her tone. It matches the determination I felt to make her mine, despite how long we've known each other.

"Now, stop stalling."

"Right..." I sigh. "I'm not sure if you've noticed, but I can be an intense guy. My ex liked to say *too* intense or attached. Clingy. Overprotective. Take your pick, Tara used it as an insult."

"I'm sorry. So, you were thinking about her?"

"I was thinking about how what I feel for you after mere days far outmatches what was between Tara and I. And I don't want to scare you off."

"You won't. The thing is... No one has ever treated me like I'm something special. The fact that I inspire such passion in you is kind of intoxicating."

"Yeah?"

"Yeah."

"Good to know." I've never considered my intensity a strength, but maybe I needed Hope to show me it could be.

I caress her back, contemplating the change of perspective.

"What's your secret, since I'm guessing it wasn't the fact that you were a virgin?"

Her muscles tense beneath my touch before releasing with a long exhale. "I'm one of the Guardian Valley heirs."

"No shit?" Of all the things Hope could have admitted to, this never even occurred to me. "Why are you staying at Vanderhorn's place rather than Serenity Ranch? They have plenty of empty cabins you could commandeer."

"I've been too overwhelmed to go over there. Brooke is my friend, but I haven't seen the other heirs since we were kids. It just seemed easier bunking at Braden's home with Carrie instead of jumping into the situation there."

"They'll love you, trust me. But I understand wanting to ease into everything. It's not every day you become an heiress and inherit a handful of strangers, too."

"You make the decision sound almost reasonable when I've been berating myself for being ridiculous."

"You're not ridiculous." I hug her closer and drop a kiss to her crown. The tangled brown strands cling to my beard. "You're protecting yourself. No one can fault you for that."

Hope yawns and snuggles her nose into the crook of my neck. "Thank you. I'm going to try to remember that."

"Why don't we table the subject for now, hmm? You've got to be exhausted after everything that's happened today."

"I don't want to miss a moment of this, though," she says through another yawn.

I gently trace the roundness of her cheek, careful not to irritate any leftover aches from being hit by an airbag.

"I'm not going anywhere, baby. Rest."

She murmurs something I don't quite catch then cuddles closer, and I revel in the trust she's given me.

Being vulnerable with her mind and body.

Staring up at the ceiling, I watch shadows from the flames dance across the beams rather than sleep.

Because I don't want to miss this either.

CHAPTER EIGHT

HOPE

"Can a girl not have one second to inwardly squeal over her good fortune?"

A BANG ON THE DOOR wakes me up. Morning light paints the floor in warm colors as I blink away the sleepy haze over my eyes and roll over. Samuel's chest rises rhythmically beneath my hand, and I take a moment to enjoy the view.

Dark hair covers his pectoral muscles, narrowing to the happy trail that leads to his cock resting against his thigh. His beard is a little fuller like he hasn't had time to trim it since our little snowed-in 'sexcation'.

Another knock on the door.

Ugh! Can a girl not have one second to inwardly squeal over her good fortune?

At first, I figured the noise came from a broken tree branch or something, but the patterned knock quickly dispelled that notion.

Samuel growls as he stretches, the move gently lifting me with the long inhale, before he stomps over to open the door.

A gust of icy snowflakes flies inside, and like that first breath out of a steaming shower, my lungs take a full breath—no longer stifled by the heat of being surrounded by Samuel.

"Braden! What are you doing here?" My fingers scramble to gather the woolen blanket around my waist, so it hides my naked chest from view.

"Carrie was worried when you never returned home and never answered any of her calls. Last night was hell, but the weather let up enough this morning that I was able to drive the snowmobile into town to see if you hunkered down at the B&B, but I found your car in a ditch instead," he explains, eyeing Samuel suspiciously. "Once I dug a hole deep enough to find it empty, I prayed you might be here rather than lost in the woods. Carrie will be happy to know you're safe, so we should get going."

"She's not going anywhere." Samuel shuts the door behind Braden and moves to stand in front of me, his arms crossed over his chest. He managed to throw on a pair of sweatpants to answer the door, but otherwise, he's barefoot and bare-chested—a sight I'd love to explore more—but it looks like my snowed-in fantasy turned reality is over.

Especially since Braden and Samuel are glaring at each other like a couple of pissed-off bulls ready to gore the other.

A tense stand-off is exactly what I wanted the morning after hours of cuddling, chatting, and making love with Samuel.

Damn Braden.

And damn the fickle weather for miraculously clearing enough for him to find me.

CHAPTER NINE

SAMUEL

"Never thought I could aspire to be someone's trophy husband..."

MONTANANS ARE USED to snow. We thrive in harsh conditions and know how to survive. So, despite yesterday's storm, there's no doubt in my mind that people are starting to move about again now that the snow has stopped falling.

Which means nothing is keeping the asshole on my doorstep from stealing Hope away.

"Hope can speak for herself," Vanderhorn says, barging into the living room.

"I'm sorry you guys were worried." Hope hops to her feet, and immediately, I stride to stand in front of her, blocking Vanderhorn from seeing her undressed state. She looks like she's been fucked all night, which is true, but Vanderhorn doesn't need to know our business.

"My phone died, and we couldn't charge it because of the power outage. Let me get dressed, and I'll ride back with you to ease Carrie's mind."

The proposition causes the possessive beast within me to roar in denial. I don't want her to leave with him. I don't want Hope to leave at all. But I can't exactly keep her prisoner here.

Hope grabs my hand as she slides in front of me. "Once I reassure Carrie that I'm safe, I'll come back, okay?"

Some of the tension eases around my shoulders. She's planning on returning to me.

For now...

Guess I'll find out if she meant everything she said about her feelings last night, or if it was just words spoken in the aftermath of surviving a traumatic event.

I pray it's the latter, because my poor heart may not recover if Hope decides she doesn't want anything more beyond our one night together.

"EARTH TO SAMUEL. YOU still in there?" Heath knocks his fist gently on my temple to get my attention. We're catching up over breakfast at his place, discussing what a bitch it'd been seeing to the horses in this shitty weather.

I slap his arm aside. "I'm listening, asshole. Your rich wife installed heaters in the stables and automatic feeders, so you got to sleep in during the blizzard. You're a lucky bastard, I get it."

"You make him sound like a gold-digging husband." Adeline, Heath's wife, giggles from across the table as she nurses their three-month-old baby. She's sweet and totally unsuited for rough ranch life, but the two of them make it work.

And it's more about love than money for my best friend.

I'm just busting his balls.

"Never thought I could aspire to be someone's trophy husband, yet here we are." Heath grins before leaning over to peck his wife on the cheek.

Samantha and Derek enter the kitchen with sheepish expressions. No doubt, the couple had been enjoying a cozy time in bed rather than dealing with guests. Technically, Samantha manages the house and cabins, cooking meals and cleaning the residences, but we all know how to fend for ourselves when she decides to take a break.

It's not like Adeline would fire her sister-in-law, especially for such a flexible job and one Samantha has been doing for years.

"Look what the cat dragged in," I say, winking at a blushing Samantha. Derek's hand squeezes her hip and goes to the cupboard to pull down two mugs.

"Shut up."

"We had to make our own pancakes this morning, sis. Wouldn't want the boss to know you're slacking on the job."

Samantha opens her mouth for a rebuttal when the doorbell rings.

"Are we expecting someone?" Addie asks.

"Not that I know of." Heath exits the kitchen and returns with the surprise guest—Hope.

I immediately stand and pull a chair out for her. It's been two days since we were snowed-in together, and true to her word, she returned to Harper's Landing, where I gave her an abbreviated tour of the ranch, including a visit with Krueger who still adores her and loathes me.

But during that time, she hadn't mentioned visiting Serenity Ranch yet.

A tremulous smile highlights Hope's nervousness, and I reach beneath the kitchen table to pat her knee. She's got this, and I've got her.

"Everyone, this is Hope Gonzalez. The fifth Foster heir," Heath says, making the introductions. The fourth heir, Ryan, rarely hangs out at the ranch after renting a place in town to be closer to his job as the hockey coach at the high school. "And look who she brought with her." He gestures behind him.

Braden fucking Vanderhorn steps inside the kitchen, and my hackles raise. What is he doing here?

"Oh my gosh, you're here!" Samantha sets her mug of coffee down to wrap Hope in an impromptu hug, ignoring the huge elephant in the room. "Brooke mentioned knowing you, but she didn't tell us you were on your way to Guardian Valley. We would have planned a welcome celebration."

"That's not necessary, though I appreciate it. I've actually been in Guardian Valley for a while. I've been staying next door at Braden's."

"Why?" Addie's brows scrunch together.

Hope readjusts her glasses, fidgeting with the plastic frames. "I wasn't ready to meet everyone yet. Nothing against you guys. It's been a lot to take in."

"That makes sense. You have to do what's right for you." Addie's concerned gaze bounces between the men in the room. She knows our troubled history.

An awkward silence falls over us, providing Vanderhorn an opportunity to speak up. His hands lift in a show of surrender.

"I come in peace. Travis, Hope, and Carrie have each given me an earful about how much of an ass I've been, specifically to you, Winters."

My brows practically hit my hairline at the roundabout apology.

"Thanks to them, I've finally seen the error of my ways, and I promise to drop the subject of buying Harper's Landing."

"About damn time," I mutter. Hope's hand covers mine on her knee, and a tiny grin plays on her lips. Seems like I have her to thank for Vanderhorn's change of heart. She mentioned saying something to her friend about his pushy behavior, but I hadn't been confident Vanderhorn would listen to anything anyone had to say.

I'm happy to be proven wrong, though.

"While dropping Hope off, I saw your truck outside and figured I should let you know that the topic is closed. Officially. Now, I'll let you all catch up." He dips his chin in farewell and leaves.

A swell of chatter erupts after his departure as if the air he'd sucked out of the room upon entry has returned tenfold.

"Congrats, man. I'm glad you won't have to deal with his bullshit anymore."

"Me, too, and it's all thanks to you." I bump Hope's shoulder with mine.

"All I did was talk to Carrie. She did most of the heavy lifting."

"Still... I'm grateful." My fingers wrap around hers and bring them to my lips so I can kiss the tips.

"Um, wait... How do you guys know each other?" Samantha asks.

Hope and I share a secret look, smug smiles teasing our mouths, before relaying the PG version of our new relationship.

It's not like any of them can judge the swiftness of our connection considering how quickly the two couples got together. But I'm relieved all the same when everyone congratulates us.

These people are my family, so their support means a lot. And now I can share that with my girl, too.

Show her that not only does she belong with me, but she belongs in Guardian Valley.

CHAPTER TEN

HOPE

"Who needs a fictional boyfriend when I've got a real fucking cowboy?"

SAMUEL GROANS BENEATH me as I ride his cock into oblivion. He was extremely grateful for my interference with Braden, and he hasn't stopped proving it from the moment we stumbled into his house kissing and stripping like a couple of horny teens.

"You feel so good, baby."

"Do I?" Teasing him, I clench my pussy around his cock and relish his grunt of pleasure.

"You're the best damn thing I've ever felt, Hope. The best damn thing I've ever had. Tell me you're planning on staying in Guardian Valley after fulfilling the one-year obligation."

Silly man.

My fingernails dig into his shoulders while I rock into him. "You couldn't force me to leave even if some other dead billionaire decided to come out of the woodwork and leave me another massive inheritance. I like Guardian Valley, and I like you."

"Thank fuck!" Samuel rolls so I'm pinned beneath him and hammers into my pussy, bouncing us on the bed until we both come with varying cries of satisfaction.

Who needs a fictional boyfriend when I've got a real fucking cowboy?

Just kidding! I'll never give up my romance novels, but they're definitely enhanced by the knowledge that I have my own protective hero to call my own.

He can be over the top at times, but I adore how obsessed he is with me. Love that I don't have to question his feelings because he makes them obvious every single day.

Stroking his bearded cheek, a happy sigh flutters free.

I finally feel like I'm home, and it's in Samuel's strong embrace.

EPILOGUE

SAMUEL

"We live an idyllic life in Guardian Valley."

HOPE'S LONG HAIR FLIES behind her as Krueger takes off in a run. Over the years, I've taught my girl everything I know about horses, and her connection with Krueger has only deepened with time.

He's mellowed out with her care, though she remains his favorite person. Something I can't blame him for.

"Hurry up if you want to win!" My wife calls back to me.

Urging my gelding to go faster, I race across the Montana plains to catch up with Hope, marveling at how lucky I am.

We live an idyllic life in Guardian Valley—full of love and family with all of the heirs, their spouses, and the children that have come.

Vanderhorn and I are even on civil-speaking terms these days. Something I never would have imagined before.

And it's all thanks to my girl. Like her name, Hope gave me a glimpse of a better future the moment I met her. She taught me that I'm not *too much* for the right person and that I don't have to hide my true self to be accepted.

I thought I wasn't meant for relationships, but that's not true. I just hadn't found the right woman yet.

Turns out, she needed to find *me* instead.

EPILOGUE TWO

HOPE

"Catastrophizing. I like it."

THE ARENA BUZZER BLASTS through the air to signal the end of the second period. A sea of blue and silver fills the bleachers, the Guardian Valley High School's mascot decorating most fans, including myself.

Samuel and I are wearing matching blue hoodies to support Ryan at his team's first hockey game and his first official test as head coach. So far, the boys are doing well—scoring two goals to the opposing team's zero.

"They look good, right?" Ryan's sister and one of my best friends, Brooke, claps her hands in time with the hype music currently playing. Travis and Samuel are busy grabbing hot cocoa for our group.

"I'm not a hockey aficionado, but yeah, I think so. I mean, they're winning, so that's encouraging."

Brooke nods and bites her lip. "You're right. I don't know why I'm so nervous. It's not like this stuff is new to me. I've attended hundreds of Ryan's games, but it's different watching him coach rather than play. I want this to work out for him, you know?"

"It will." I wrap an arm around Brooke's shoulders and hug her to my side. "Even if this game takes a turn, there are plenty more on the schedule. And based on what he's shared about the team's past, I doubt he can do much worse."

"Catastrophizing. I like it." Brooke grins. It's reminiscent of her brother's, and I glance down at the ice to see the boys huddled around him as he goes over strategies for the next period.

I've known Ryan for as long as I've known Brooke, and there's no doubt in my mind that he'll be fine.

Ryan is great with kids of all ages. They're usually in awe of him because he used to be a professional hockey player, but he's also really easygoing. Even with my history of awkwardness with men, I never felt that way with Ryan. He made it easy to be friends.

"See #47?" Brooke points to a player sitting on the team bench. "Ryan says that kid could be the next Crosby."

I have no clue who that is, but if Ryan can take #47 under his wing and make his dreams come true, then I'm here for it.

After all, that's what Guardian Valley has done for me—made my dreams come true by gifting me with a rugged cowboy who's obsessed with me and a found family of people who are always in my corner.

The third period starts after the men return with our drinks, and I feel a kiss on the top of my head. Snuggling into Samuel's side, a wave of gratitude washes over me.

Life doesn't get any better than this.

Don't miss Brooke's brother, Ryan, in *Montana Guardian*!

Get up-to-date book information and stay connected with Hallie Bennett here[1]!

---

1. https://www.thearrowedheart.com/hallie-bennett

THANKS FOR READING & DON'T FORGET TO RATE/ REVIEW!

Please consider leaving a rating/review. Ratings & reviews are the #1 way to support an indie author like me.
The more reviews, the more my books are shown to other potential readers!
And they serve as guides to readers on whether or not to take a chance on an indie author.
I appreciate your support!
XO, Hallie

ABOUT THE AUTHOR

Hallie prefers steamy, instalove stories where curvy girls are claimed by filthy-talking heroes. And when she ran out of reading material, she decided to write her own stories. If you want a quick, hot read, she's your girl!